Mixed-Up Magic

Written by Michael Pellowski
Illustrated by Doug Cushman

Troll Associate

Library of Congress Cataloging-in-Publication Data

Pellowski, Michael.
  Mixed-up magic / written by Michael Pellowski; illustrated by
Doug Cushman.
      p.   cm.—(Fiddlesticks)
  Summary: Waldo the wizard discovers some wacky changes in his
powers after his clumsy assistant drops Waldo's magic wand.
  ISBN 0-8167-1327-8 (lib. bdg.)   ISBN 0-8167-1328-6 (pbk.)
  [1. Wizards—Fiction.   2. Magic—Fiction.]   I. Cushman, Doug,
ill.   II. Title.   III. Series.
  PZ7.P3656Mi 1989
  [E]—dc19   88-1312

In a land of dragons, knights, and magic lived a little wizard named Waldo. Waldo knew every magic spell there was to know. He could turn a terrible thunderstorm into a shower of spring flowers. He could change a mean ogre into a cuddly bunny. He could even make a mountain vanish and reappear.

With the help of his wondrous magic wand, there wasn't a trick Waldo couldn't do. And because he was so kindly, Waldo the wizard always used his magic to do good deeds.

Waldo lived in a cozy cave with his helper, Dimwitty. Most of the time Dimwitty did a very good job. He helped with magic potions. He kept Waldo's wizard hat neat and clean. And most important of all, he took good care of Waldo's magic wand.

But at other times, Dimwitty was just a bit clumsy. He spilled a skunk potion and made the cave smell. Once he sat on Waldo's hat and squashed it flat. And not very often—but once in a while—he was careless with the wizard's magic wand.

"What a great day," Waldo said to his helper early one morning. Waldo looked out the window. "The sun is shining brightly. The sky is clear and blue. It's a good day to work magic."

Dimwitty nodded. "And there's a lot of magic work to do today," Dimwitty told the wizard. "Today is the Elf Queen's birthday. You also have to help King Morgan. *And* there is a dragon to fight."

"I know," said Waldo. "Today will be a very busy day."

"I might as well get to work," the wizard said. "Dimwitty, please run and fetch my magic wand."

Dimwitty bowed politely. "Yes, wizard," he said, and away he rushed.

Dimwitty ran to where the wand was kept. Carefully, he picked it up. With the wand in his hands he hurried back to the wizard. He didn't see the stool in his path.

"Yipes," yelled Dimwitty, as he tumbled forward.

Crash!

Down went Dimwitty.

Up in the air went the wand.

When it came down, it hit the floor hard.

Ka-plop!

Off popped the magic star from the tip of the wand.

"Oh no," cried Dimwitty when he saw the wand in two pieces. "What am I going to do? The wizard will be so angry he'll never let me touch the wand again."

Dimwitty scooped up the broken wand. He looked at it very closely. It wasn't really broken. The star had just popped off the end of the wand.

"Maybe I can stick the star back on," Dimwitty said.

Dimwitty fit the two pieces together. He pushed the star back on the end of the wand.

"There," he said happily. "Now the wizard will never know the difference. The wand is as good as new."

And away he ran.

The wand did look perfect. But it really
wasn't as good as new. In fact, it wasn't fixed
at all. Dimwitty had mixed up the ends of
the wand. He'd put the star on the wrong
end of the stick. The magic star was on
backwards! The wand was upside down.
What kind of magic would the wand work
now?

"Here is your wand, sir," said Dimwitty.

"Thank you," Waldo answered. He put on his pointed hat and took the wand from his helper. Waldo never noticed that there was something a little different about his magic wand.

Waldo started out of his cave.

"See what you can do about getting rid of those pesky mice," Waldo said to Dimwitty. "They keep getting in the bread cupboard."

"I will," Dimwitty promised. "Have a good day!"

Waldo walked off into the enchanted forest.

Waldo hadn't walked far when he met a beautiful princess. She was on her way to see the wizard.

"I need your help," she told Waldo. The princess held out her hand. In it was a big, green frog. "A wicked witch changed a handsome prince into this frog," she sobbed. "Now we can't be wed."

"Please help us," croaked the frog.

The kindly wizard smiled. "A princess cannot marry a frog," he agreed. "I will fix everything." And he raised his magic wand.

"*Ala-ka-zam!*" Waldo cried, waving the wand.

Ka-boom!

There was a blinding flash. When the smoke cleared, Waldo couldn't believe his eyes. The frog prince hadn't changed at all. He was still a frog. But the princess had changed. Now she was a frog, too. What mixed-up magic was this?

"Hey! We're both frogs!" said the prince.

"Isn't it wonderful?" said the princess. "A princess can't marry a frog. But a frog can marry a frog."

"That's right," said the prince. "Thank you, wizard." And away hopped the happy frogs.

Waldo was confused. He knew something had gone wrong. He had meant to change the frog prince back into a man. But the magic had gotten mixed up.

"I'll figure it out later," said Waldo. "The frogs are happy, and I'm late for the Elf Queen's birthday party."

Still puzzled, the wizard rushed off.

The Elf Queen was glad to see Waldo when he arrived at her castle. Waldo and the queen were very good friends.

"I have a special present for your birthday," the wizard told the queen. Two elves brought in a huge mirror.

"What kind of present is that?" asked the Elf Queen. "That's my old mirror."

"I'm going to make it a magic mirror,"
explained Waldo. He tapped his wand on the
mirror three times.

"*Shazam!*" he shouted.

The mirror began to glow. Waldo smiled
proudly. "No matter when you use this
mirror," said Waldo, "you will never look
old. In the mirror you will always look as
young and beautiful as you do today."

"What a thoughtful gift," exclaimed the queen. She rushed up to the mirror and stared into the glowing glass.

What a shock!

The beautiful elf looked very strange in the mirror. Her neck and legs were long and skinny. Her body was wide. Her feet were big. And her head was pointed!

The wand had changed the glass into a fun-house mirror.

When Waldo saw the Elf Queen's reflection, he didn't know what to do. "How did that happen?" he wondered. "And what will the queen say?" The wizard swallowed hard and waited.

The Elf Queen stared at the mirror. She glanced at Waldo. Then she looked back into the mirror.

Suddenly, she burst out laughing. "What a great present," she chuckled. "And what a funny joke to play on me. Waldo, you are wonderful and tricky, too."

The Elf Queen gave Waldo a big hug. Waldo didn't say a word. He just smiled meekly as each of the elves looked in the mirror and laughed.

When Waldo left the party, he was more puzzled than ever. What was wrong? Was he losing his magical power?

The little wizard hoped his magic would work when he met King Morgan. King Morgan's knights were going to chase a mean giant out of the land. And to do that, they needed help from Waldo.

"Welcome, Waldo," said King Morgan
when the wizard arrived. "We've been
waiting for you."

King Morgan and his knights had gathered
in a big field. The knights were mounted on
steeds and dressed for battle. They wore
armor and carried swords.

"Where is the mean giant?" Waldo asked.

Waldo's question was quickly answered. Thundering footsteps echoed out of a nearby valley.

THUMP! THUMP! THUMP!

"The giant is coming!" cried the king to his knights. "Prepare to charge."

Waldo lifted his wand and pointed it at the knights. "I will use my wand to make your swords magic," he cried. "With magic swords you will be able to frighten the giant away."

Waldo waved his wand.

"Presto-change-o!" he shouted.

Zing!

The magic began to work. The knights' swords began to shine bright yellow.

The mean giant stepped out of the valley and stared at the knights. Loudly, he began to laugh.

The knights looked at their swords. Waldo's magic had changed their weapons into huge, yellow bananas!

"I'll get you!" the giant yelled, as he charged.

Without weapons, the knights were defenseless. They threw down their banana swords and rode away as fast as they could.

The giant followed. He stepped on the big bananas—and slipped.

"Whoa!" cried the giant as he flew into the air. Head over heels he went. *Thud!* The giant hit the ground so hard the earth shook. He knocked himself senseless.

"Great work, Waldo!" shouted King Morgan. "The giant is helpless. We'll tie him up and force him to leave our land forever. Your magic is truly amazing!"

Waldo didn't answer. What could he say? He had only stopped the giant by accident. He couldn't tell anyone about his puzzling magic.

As the knights tied up the giant, Waldo slipped away. Quietly, he sneaked off into the woods. He wanted to go home, but he couldn't. There was still a dragon to fight.

When Waldo reached the cave of the fire-breathing dragon, he was worried. He knew his magic wasn't working right—and he didn't know why.

But he had promised everyone he'd get rid of the dragon. He couldn't let it go on burning villages and forests. Mixed-up magic or not, something had to be done.

Suddenly, Waldo heard a frightening noise from deep in the cave. *Growlll! Hissss!* The dragon was coming out!

Waldo glanced at his wand and gulped. Would his magic work this time?

Out came the big scaly dragon. He saw
the little wizard and licked his lips. Opening
his mouth, the dragon shot a stream of fire at
Waldo.

"I'll give that dragon some of his own medicine," said Waldo. *"Beam-sola-bim. Send a fireball back at him!"* And he waved his magic wand.

But it wasn't a giant fireball Waldo sent
hurling at the dragon. It was a huge snowball
instead. When the dragon opened his mouth
to breathe more flames, in went the snowball.

"*Gulp!*" said the dragon.

Sisssst! The giant snowball melted. It put
out the dragon's fire forever. And it gave him
a super bellyache, too.

Moaning and groaning, the soggy dragon
dragged himself back into the cave.

"So much for dragons," said Waldo,
looking at his wand in a puzzled way.
"Now I can go home."

As he walked, Waldo thought about everything that had happened. He knew he was lucky it had worked out all right. But he *had* to figure out what was going on.

On his way home, Waldo took a short cut by the river. Unfortunately, a flood had washed away the bridge. There was no way for the wizard to get to the other side.

Waldo stopped on the river bank and
looked at his wand. "Oh well! Here goes
nothing," he said. "Maybe my magic will
work this time."

Waldo tapped himself on the head with
the wand. *"Presto-change-o,"* he said.
"Turn me into a big bird so I can fly across
the river."

Shazam! There was a bright flash.

"It worked," Waldo cried. "I'm a big bird." He jumped into the air. True, Waldo was a big bird, but the magic was mixed up again. Waldo had changed into an ostrich. An ostrich cannot fly.

Ker-splash! Into the river went Waldo.

Minutes later, a very wet ostrich climbed out on the other side of the river.

"I'm washed up as a wizard," said Waldo sadly.

He tapped himself once again with the wand. This time, for an unexplainable reason, the magic worked. Waldo changed back into himself. Discouraged and dripping wet, he headed for home.

Dimwitty was waiting at the door when Waldo arrived. "Wizard, I couldn't get rid of the mice," cried Dimwitty.

Waldo handed Dimwitty the wand. "Use this to make a mousetrap," he sighed. "I'm not good at magic anymore. You're promoted from helper to wizard."

Dimwitty didn't want to be a wizard, but he took the wand and went into the next room.

Zap! Flash!

Waldo heard Dimwitty doing magic.

Squeak! Squeak! Squeak! Suddenly, dozens of frightened mice ran by Waldo and out of the cave.

"Dimwitty's magic must have worked," said Waldo. He went off to see the new wizard.

When Waldo entered the next room, he
didn't find Dimwitty. What he found was a
giant cat that looked like Dimwitty.

"Instead of making a mousetrap, the wand
turned me into a cat," mewed Dimwitty.
"Something must be wrong with the wand."

"The wand!" cried Waldo. He rushed over to Dimwitty and picked up the wand. Carefully, he looked over every inch of it.

"The star is on upside down," he said at last. "The wand is backwards! There is nothing wrong with my powers. It's the wand that is mixed up!"

Quickly, Waldo took the wand apart and
fixed it. Once it was ready, he was able to
change Dimwitty back to normal. Waldo was
so happy to have his powers back, he didn't
even get angry when Dimwitty explained
about dropping the wand.

"Just be careful from now on," cautioned
Waldo, as they walked into the next room.

Waldo was surprised to see two green frogs waiting for him. They were the prince and princess.

"We don't want to be frogs, after all," said the prince.

"Can you please change us back?" begged the princess.

Waldo looked at his wand and nodded. *"Ala-ka-zam!"* shouted the wizard, waving the wand.

Poof! Instantly, the frogs vanished. Before the wizard stood a handsome prince and a beautiful princess.

"Thank you," said the prince.

"Waldo, you are a great wizard," said the princess.

Waldo smiled proudly.

Waldo turned to Dimwitty. "Yes, I am still a great wizard after all, and you are a great wizard's helper," he said.

Dimwitty smiled. He liked being Waldo's helper.

Waldo handed Dimwitty the magic wand. "Please put this away," he said. "And try not to drop it. I've had enough mixed-up magic for one day!"

Dimwitty took the wand and carefully, very carefully, walked away.